MW01048080

**Redford Township District Library**
**25320 West Six Mile Road**
**Redford, MI 48240**

**www.redford.lib.mi.us**

**Hours:**

**Mon–Thur 10–8:30**
**Fri–Sat  10–5**
**Sunday (School Year) 12–5**

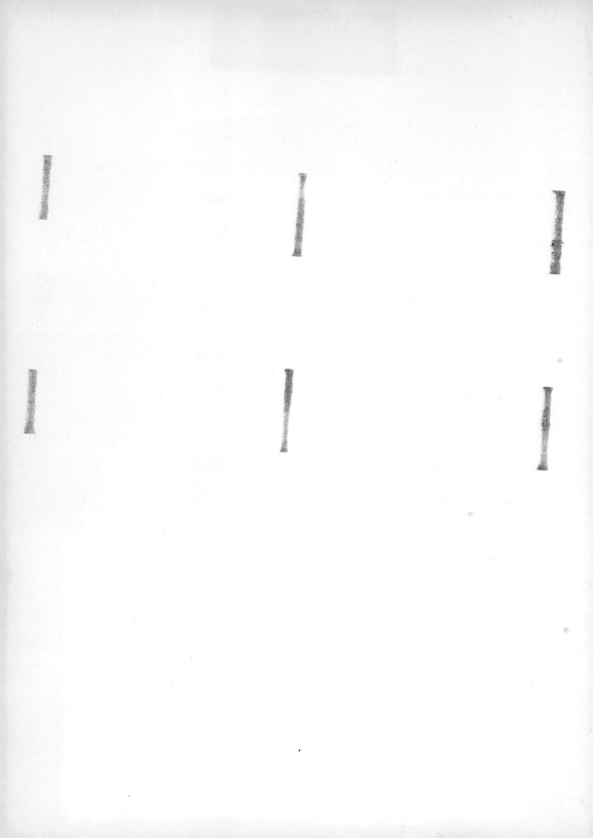

*The Seven Stone*

# The Seven Stone

by
Mary Francis Shura

*illustrated by Dale Payson*

HOLIDAY HOUSE/NEW YORK

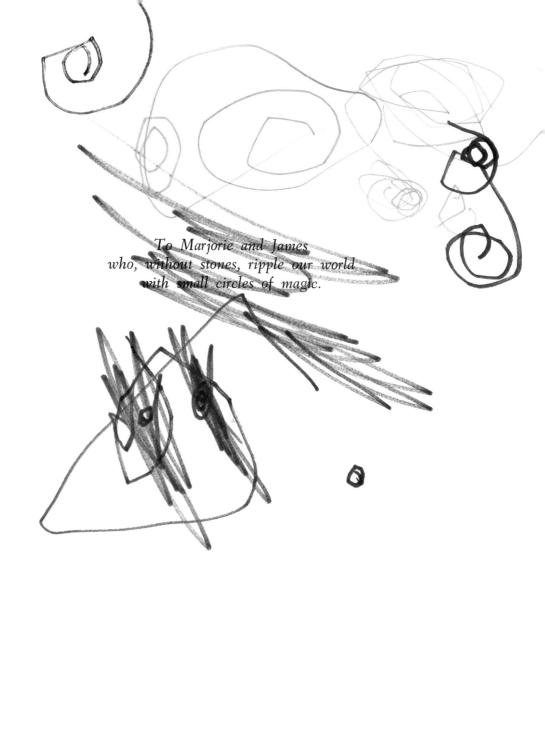

To Marjorie and James
who, without stones, ripple our world
with small circles of magic.

Table of Contents

# ❦ *Once A Magpie*

Even before Tibbie came, that day had been one of the most awful days in Maggie Underwood's whole life. The awful part began when Maggie first got to school. She had run up to Linda and the others on the playground just like any other day.

But instead of greeting her and telling her how pretty she looked in her blue dress with the white stars on the collar, Linda had looked at her blankly and turned away. Then the others turned away too.

Because Maggie wasn't as bold as Linda or Shelley, she couldn't come right out and ask what was the matter. Instead she felt scared, and knew that if she didn't get away by herself really fast, she would cry.

Maggie dragged away unhappily, wishing it wasn't almost time for the bell. When it rang she would have to go and sit in the classroom with them and they would sneer at her like they had at Betty Ann.

Betty Ann used to be in the crowd too. Then one day Linda and the others decided they didn't like her anymore. "She's fat and ugly and eats like a pig with her fingers," Linda said.

Anyone could see that Betty Ann was fat but she wasn't ugly at all and Maggie had eaten lunch with her enough times to know that her table manners were just as good as anyone else's. The only difference was that she ate twice as much.

But Maggie had gone along with the rest, knowing they were being unfair but dreading that awful feeling of being shut out of the crowd if she didn't act the way they did.

Maggie couldn't explain to anyone what it meant to be "in" with Linda and the others. She had tried to explain it to her brother, Jason, when they first began to include her in their fun, and he had been very strange about it.

Jason was fifteen and a half and already had his permit to learn to drive. His face was stubbly with little nicked places where he made mistakes shaving and his voice was almost as deep as that of Maggie's Dad, but best of all he didn't mind listening to her.

When Maggie tried to tell him about Linda and the others, he only frowned a little and asked, "What's so big about them?"

"Because when you're in, it's just wonderful, and when you aren't, you feel like something is wrong with you."

He looked at her a moment and slipped a penny from his pocket. He laid it on his open palm and asked, "What's that?"

"A penny, silly," she giggled.

He tossed the penny onto the floor of the porch where it clinked musically. Jefferson Dog ran over to inspect it quickly before sniffing and turning away.

"Now what is it?" Jason asked.

"It's still a penny," Maggie replied, picking it up.

"Just remember that," he said, ruffling her hair. "Once a Magpie, always a Magpie . . . in or out. Okay?"

Because she knew he wouldn't understand, she never talked to Jason again about the crowd. She especially didn't mention what they did to Betty Ann.

And today it was her turn to be treated badly. "It isn't fair," Maggie told herself fiercely. "I'm not even fat or anything."

The clangor of the bell sent her racing to her room but that miserable hollow feeling was still inside her when she slipped into her seat.

The morning dragged. A flood of sunshine slanted across the desks and made golden lines on the floor. Maggie stared at the lines of light to keep from having to look at anyone. She noticed that the fish were darting about in the aquarium against the wall and Maggie watched the fronds of the water plants sway as they swam past. She couldn't bear to look above the fish tank to where Linda's name was written in gold chalk as the champion speller, any more than she could stand to look at her friends' faces and have them look away quickly as if her eyes would soil them.

Math was finally over and they got their books out for reading. It was then that the new girl came, right between math and reading with the sun still gleaming and Miss Barrow nudging the chairs around to make the two tables ready for the reading groups.

The assistant principal, Miss Hopkins, brought the new girl to the door. Everyone turned to stare, and after only a moment of silence, a low excited buzzing began.

She was tiny, smaller even than Suki Dong, who had always been the smallest girl in their room. Her dress was dark blue and very long and full. Instead of sneakers or shoes, she was wearing little hiking boots that laced up on the outside with hooks instead of holes.

But it was her face that Maggie stared at. Her hair, which was very shiny and dark, was parted in the middle and hung straight to her waist. Her face was slender and pointed at the chin and her eyes were very dark, and shining too, like her hair.

"We have a new student for you, Miss Barrow," Miss Hopkins said, in that slightly higher voice she always used when children were around. "This is Tibbie Reid, and she has been assigned to your room."

Maggie studied Tibbie's face only the barest moment before glancing away. She wondered what Linda and the others were thinking, how they were looking at the new girl. But with them so mad at her, she didn't dare look at their faces to see.

Once upon a time Maggie's school had had a dress code. Nobody had been allowed to wear slacks or long dresses or shorts to

classes. Now the dress code had been taken away. Sometimes the girls in the older grades wore long dresses and Indian-style headbands, but Maggie knew that Linda and the others always giggled and pointed and called them "hippies" when they dressed like that.

But Tibbie Reid didn't seem to be afraid of looking at anyone.

Her round dark eyes dived like birds about the room, looking and seeing so sharply that it scared Maggie. When Tibbie's eyes met Maggie's, Maggie looked down. Maggie felt as if Tibbie could see right down inside her, down to where Maggie was hiding that big ball of hurt over Linda and the others.

"Welcome, Tibbie," Miss Barrow said heartily, as if she too had been surprised by the dark shadow of a child at the door. "Come in, we'll find you a desk and chair."

Of course Miss Barrow didn't have to *find* a chair and desk for Tibbie, but Miss Barrow always talked like that, making things sound more important or difficult than they really were. The last seat at the end of the second row had been empty since the first day of school. Tibbie saw the vacant seat immediately and walked calmly over to it and sat down.

With quite a bit of whispering and some giggling, Tibbie's desk was equipped with books and workbooks, and class started again.

All that time the children kept staring at Tibbie and she stared right back at them, not smiling, not scared, just firm . . . as if, Maggie thought, she was proving they couldn't make any holes in her with their eyes.

"Now, about reading class," Miss Barrow said. She glanced about the room, smiling. "Maggie, why don't you make it your responsibility to help Tibbie until she gets used to our school? Be sure and show her the library during recess so she can check out some extra-credit books."

Tibbie spoke for the first time. Her voice was low and sort of forceful, as if she were defending herself against someone.

"I learn my way around fast," she said firmly.

Miss Barrow looked faintly surprised, but then she smiled. "I'm sure you do, Tibbie. But it's nice to have a sort of friend in a new place, like a hostess."

Tibbie only frowned deeper. Maggie sat in her chair for a long minute. She really dreaded having to go get Tibbie and show her around. Why hadn't Miss Barrow picked somebody else to have to look into that strange girl's face and spend all that time with her?

When almost everyone else was on the way to the reading tables, Maggie got up slowly. Tibbie stared back at her with those hard, dark eyes when Maggie stood by her desk.

"I usually pick my own friends," she said coldly, as if Maggie had done something insulting just by obeying the teacher.

Maggie silently led Tibbie to the first reading group, where Linda and the others had already taken their seats. Chairs shuffled and scraped as people sat down.

The teacher didn't hear Linda's amused whisper as Maggie and Tibbie sat down across from her. "Birds of a feather," she chanted mockingly, but very softly so that only the people at their table could hear.

When the giggles quieted, Maggie could feel Tibbie next to her like a resentful icicle. From the fish tank behind them came the slow soft regularity of air bubbles breaking through the water's surface.

Maggie had never felt so lonely and miserable in all her life.

# ⚙ *Tibbie*

Maggie really wasn't sorry to miss the morning recess. If she didn't have to show the new girl around, she would be out there on the playground all by herself, with Linda and the others snubbing her.

"We'll do the library first," Maggie announced.

"Okay, I guess," Tibbie said, shrugging. "Only I already have hundreds of books in my room at home."

Hundreds. Maggie repeated the word to herself without believing Tibbie, but she didn't say anything.

One of the older grades was leaving the library as Maggie and Tibbie went in. Some of the big girls stopped and stared at Tibbie a moment before glancing at Maggie. As they walked away, Maggie could feel them still looking back at them. She felt embarrassed, and mad at herself at the same time, for caring.

Maggie pretended to browse through the magazines while Tibbie chose two books. She told herself defensively that Miss Barrow hadn't said that she had to stay with the new girl every minute.

"I found two that aren't half bad," Tibbie said with satisfaction. "Maybe this place will be okay."

When Maggie didn't answer, Tibbie looked at her sharply. "Don't you like to read or something?"

"Sure I like to read," Maggie said.

"What kind of books?" Tibbie asked.

"Horse stories and mysteries," Maggie said. "If they're not too scary, that is."

"What are you going to be when you get big?" Tibbie asked.

"An airline stewardess," Maggie confessed. "I love to fly."

Tibbie laughed without smiling, a funny short laugh that ended very quickly. "I'm going to fly someday too, but not that way. I'm going to be a witch."

Maggie knew she should say something but she was too surprised to think of anything.

"In fact I already *am* a witch," Tibbie said crossly, as if Maggie had contradicted her. "I have a black cat that is my familiar and a seven stone of my own and I can make spells."

Maggie stared at her but turned away quickly at the angry look on Tibbie's face.

"I don't even know what some of those words mean," Maggie said.

"The seven stone?" Tibbie asked.

Maggie nodded, "And that part about the cat."

"Witches know a lot of things that regular people don't," Tibbie explained a little haughtily. "They believe that a little girl really gets a mind of her own when she gets to be seven years old. On her seventh birthday she gets a special stone and then she carries it always. . . ."

Her voice trailed off as she handed the books to Maggie without even a "please." She dug in the pocket of her dress for a minute. Maggie stared at the stone that Tibbie held out grandly in the palm of her hand.

The stone was a pale blueish gray and so perfectly round and flat that it lay in Tibbie's hand as if it had grown there. On it was

painted a strange sign that looked vaguely familiar but Maggie couldn't think where she had seen it before. It was really rather like a small tree with all the upper branches gone.

"That's my own sign," Tibbie said proudly, as if she were reading Maggie's mind. "Virginia made it for me. I'd never go anywhere without it. I am always safe and lucky when I have it with me."

Maggie handed Tibbie her books and walked on quickly. "I'll show you where we eat lunch."

Tibble had to skip an extra couple of steps to catch up with Maggie. "Boy, it's no wonder you don't have any friends and nobody likes you!" she said, a little out of breath from catching up.

"I do *so* have friends," Maggie said quickly, being careful not to look at Tibbie.

Tibbie stopped. "Not in school, you don't. I watched all morning. Nobody looks over at you to giggle when things happen and nobody whispers to you when they pass and they talk about you behind your back."

"I used to have friends. Even yesterday I had lots of friends," Maggie said miserably. "Today they're all just mad at me."

"For no reason?" Tibbie asked.

"No reason that I know of," Maggie admitted.

Tibbie twisted her mouth a funny way, then she nodded wisely. "I know about things like that," she said, and then continued. "It's just too bad that you're not a witch like me with a stone that protects you so that people would be afraid to turn on you like that."

"Did you have friends where you came from?" Maggie asked, suddenly curious.

"Some times, some places," Tibbie replied dreamily. "We move around a lot. I've been in Vermont and Colorado, and Arizona, and even in California. . . ." She wiggled her nose. "But I didn't much like it there."

"But this is California," Maggie said.

"I know that, silly," Tibbie said sharply. "But Mill Valley is different. It's not half bad. When I go to bed at night I can hear the deer eating outside my windows and the sea fog wraps my room in its hands."

"How come you move around so much?" Maggie asked. Her family had moved once, when Jason was little, long before she was born. But she had lived all her life on the same street, with the same room. Her family had even had the same dog all her life because Jefferson Dog had been bought for Jason before she was born.

"Virginia gets restless," Tibbie said quietly.

Maggie very much wanted to ask who Virginia might be but recess time was over. She and Tibbie both hurried toward their room.

They didn't hurry fast enough. Almost everyone was there already and they stared and tittered when Maggie and Tibbie came in the door. Maggie felt miserable, remembering that even a brand-new girl had noticed that she hadn't a single friend in that whole classroom.

Geography was hard for Maggie. She always read the pages that Miss Barrow assigned but it was so boring that she had trouble remembering things. The section they were in now was all about different kinds of climates and terrain. Maggie wasn't really interested in weather unless it was happening. She liked matching clothes to her pink slicker and hat when it rained, and she liked going over to Stinson Beach when it was hot, but just looking at big maps that showed how high the mountains were and how the winds blew didn't seem interesting to her.

"Yesterday we talked about deserts and the kind of weather they have in desert country," Miss Barrow said. "Can anyone tell us what kind of weather we have here in Mill Valley and along the California coast?"

Hands shot up all over the room.

"Rainy in the winter and dry in the summer," Albert said.

Miss Barrow nodded approvingly. "There is a particular kind

of plant growth on slopes where the water is sparse for much of the year. I'll give you a clue. Something about this terrain is valuable in water conservation and preventing soil erosion during the rainy times. Can you tell us what land like this is called?"

She paused a moment as the children exchanged glances and Maggie thought very hard. "It is a long hard word," she added, as if that would be a helpful clue.

Only Tibbie's hand was up.

"Can you tell us, Tibbie?" Miss Barrow asked hesitantly.

"Chaparral," Tibbie said firmly.

"That's horse country for grazing," Timmy corrected out loud without even putting his hand up. He said it in that funny way that Maggie always thought of as a "girls are dumb" tone.

"They grazed cattle here for a long time," Tibbie answered in a superior way. "In fact, that's almost all they *did* do before the gold rush."

"That's goofy," Matthew scoffed. "There weren't even enough people out here to eat all that meat."

"Nobody said they grew them for meat," Tibbie said scathingly. "They grew them for leather and tallow. That was before electricity, as you might or might not know."

"Children," Miss Barrow stilled them firmly. "Tibbie is right. She is talking about the early Spanish times and that is how it was. How do you happen to know so much about early California history, Tibbie?"

"I know a lot of things," Tibbie said calmly. "I have a book about it in my room and maps of all the countries that tell about their climates and things."

There was a kind of calm conceit about the way she said this that made Maggie cringe. Maggie felt that Miss Barrow didn't like Tibbie's tone either from the way she went right on talking about chaparrals and how the roots of the small trees hold water without even glancing at Tibbie again.

As the class period went on, Maggie could sense the resentment that everyone felt toward Tibbie. It wasn't that they were all that wild about Timmy or Matthew, who had contradicted Tibbie, but there was just something so smart-alecky about the way Tibbie said things that nobody could stand it.

"I want school to be over," Maggie told herself unhappily, "so I can go home."

But the morning dragged wearily on. After ever so long, it was finally time for lunch. Feeling the glances of the other kids like strings tied to her own back, Maggie led Tibbie to an empty bench to eat lunch. She felt funny sitting on the bench. This was the same bench that Betty Ann had always sat on to eat her lunch after Linda and the others shut her out. Maggie had been glad when Betty Ann's father had been transferred to Sacramento and Betty Ann moved away. It always made her feel bad to see Betty Ann sitting there by herself eating too much lunch alone and not even looking up at anyone who went by.

From the corner of her eye she could see Linda and the others fluffing their skirts out and opening their lunch bags and chattering happily with amused little glances at her and Tibbie.

Maggie had a peanut butter and marshmallow creme sandwich, crinkled potato chips, and a handful of homemade oatmeal cookies with raisins.

Tibbie had a white container like those used for ice cream. She also had a green plastic spoon and two apples, one red and one green.

"This is goat milk yoghurt," Tibbie said proudly. "The kind that comes from cows makes me get red and puff up."

"I never heard of goat milk yoghurt," Maggie admitted.

"Virginia could make the very best of all," Tibbie said. "But Virginia could do anything the best. She can sew dresses even better than this. She weaves material on a loom sometimes and paints pictures better than any artist."

After her yoghurt was finished, Tibbie took a cookie that Maggie offered her. Maggie wasn't hungry somehow, and anyway, everything she tried to swallow stuck in her throat.

"You really did well in geography today," Maggie said, to change the subject.

"I do real well in school all the time," Tibbie said placidly. "That's because I really like to learn. Someday I am going to know everything in the whole wide world. That's why I like my room so well."

"Tell me about your room," Maggie said.

"It's really big," Tibbie said proudly. "Bigger than some whole houses. I've got books in it . . . hundreds of books, and posters about things I like and a lot of maps that Bill got for me. I can roller skate out in the middle and there is a door in the roof that I can open when it isn't raining and I can see stars from my bed."

When .Maggie didn't say anything, Tibbie added, "I study stars so I can tell what constellations they are in. That is very important for a witch to know."

"Where is your house?" Maggie asked suddenly. She was sure that Tibbie was making it all up. Whoever heard of a room that was big enough to roller skate in and all?

Tibbie turned her dark eyes on Maggie. "You know that road that goes over the mountain to the ocean?" Maggie nodded. "Well, halfway up that hill is a road that goes off into the woods. At the very end of that road is my house. The house has porches all around and lots of trees. But my room is the privatest and biggest on the whole place."

Maggie knew the ocean road and the smaller road that went off from it into the woods, but she had never gone up that smaller road. It looked scary to pass because giant eucalyptus trees hid everything from the sun, and the brambles and buckbrush looked prickly and forbidding. Maggie had heard her mother and Jason talk about that road. They said there was a commune back in there.

Maggie listened carefully when her mother said the word "commune." Usually when her mother used a strange word, Maggie could tell how her mother felt about the thing by the way she said the word, with disapproval or pleasure. She couldn't tell what her mother was thinking that time. It sounded almost as if her mother were confused and asking a question when she said the word.

Maggie wasn't very sure in her own mind what a commune was either so she understood that. The word made her think of a lot of things at once . . . mostly hippie things. She thought of the long-haired men with beards, the girls who hitchhiked around Mill Valley, sometimes with little babies tied to their hips. But mostly she thought of the magnificent truck she had seen in the Fourth of July parade. It was immense and was decorated all over with statues and flowers and jewels and ornaments so that she couldn't even believe her own eyes while she was looking at it go by.

"Do you live there with Virginia?" Maggie asked.

Tibbie turned toward Maggie with a sudden fierceness. Maggie was startled by the flashing look of anger and hurt that Tibbie's eyes held and she felt scared. Then Tibbie kind of relaxed and looked down at her boots.

"I live there with lots of people," she said quietly. "With Bill and Carole and Bob and Stanley and their goats and a girl named Tricia who throws pots."

Back at her desk, Maggie sat and frowned thoughtfully. Tibbie's house didn't seem real to her at all. Every once in a while she sneaked a look back at Tibbie who bent over her desk working in a tight little crouch. Her long dark hair hung over her unsmiling face and Maggie tried to imagine what it would be like to live with someone who threw pots. It was too much, that was all.

She sighed and went back to watching the clock hands move slowly toward the time when she could go home to Jason and Jefferson Dog and her own little room that was barely big enough for her bedroom furniture and her toys, much less a place to roller skate!

# ❧ A Chance for Tibbie

When Maggie finally escaped to her home she found her brother Jason lying under the car out in the driveway. He was on his back doing something to the underneath of the car.

Maggie squatted on the driveway and peered in at him.

She wanted to talk to him so much that she couldn't even start with the first word. Jason must have figured that out because he wormed out from under the car and sat up by her.

"Problems, Magpie?" he asked.

Maggie squinched her shoulders. "Maybe just questions," she replied finally.

"Shoot," he ordered. He wiped the grease from his hands with a big rag without looking at her because he knew she couldn't talk when people stared.

"Why would somebody that didn't even know you be mean to you?" she finally asked.

"A stranger?"

She nodded. "A new girl at school."

"Really mean or just rude?"

"Well, maybe just rude," Maggie admitted. "And hard like."

Jason stared off across the privet hedge a minute and said, "Maybe she was just trying to beat you to it."

"But I wasn't going to be rude to her," Maggie protested.

Jason laughed a little. "How would she know that?" He thumped Maggie's shoulder with his arm.

Then Jason slid back under the car. His voice came thick and muffled beneath the little chinking sounds he was making with a tool.

"Outside of rude, how is she?"

Maggie squatted low to watch him. When she tried to explain Tibbie with words, they didn't seem to come out right.

"She wears funny long clothes like a hippie and says she is a witch and she has lived all over."

A funny grumbling sound came instead of an answer and Maggie went on. "She lives in that place that Mother said was a commune with a lot of other people. Jason," she paused because she knew it sounded funny, "why would anyone want to throw pots?"

The grumble changed into a roar of laughter and Jason stuck his head out to grin at her.

"That's really good, Maggie! Throwing a pot means making pottery on a wheel . . . a real potter's wheel. It's an art and really great to watch. But it sounds pretty ferocious the way you said it."

Maggie didn't like it when Jason laughed at her and she sat very still. He looked at her a moment, then said quietly, "Give the kid a chance, Maggie."

"But Jason, I think she lies a lot," Maggie almost whispered.

"Possibly," Jason nodded. Then his voice changed. He spoke a little louder and rather gaily. "Whatever you fix yourself for a snack, fix me double, will you?"

"Double what?" she asked, feeling very grown-up and important to be asked to fix food for Jason.

"Anything but a mustard sandwich," he kidded.

"I quit eating them last year," she reminded him crossly, getting up. "Now I like peanut butter and marshmallow creme."

"Sold," he said. "And heavy on the creme." Then he slid back under the car.

Maggie was careful not to get to school too early on Thursday. She didn't really know who she wanted to avoid most . . . Linda and the others or Tibbie. She only knew she didn't want any extra time on the playground that morning.

The minute she stepped inside the room, she saw Tibbie's eyes on her face. She was conscious of the other kids watching her too. Linda and the others were watching to see what she would do.

Maggie wanted to walk around Tibbie's desk and say "Hi" to her. Jason had said to give Tibbie a chance. But she couldn't force herself to do it. Instead she walked to her desk the quickest way. She did smile at Tibbie, a quick shy quirk of a smile that creased her cheek only a minute and then disappeared. Tibbie didn't smile back. She just stared at Maggie, her eyes knowing and hard.

That whole day was unbelievable to Maggie. If somebody set out to make everybody hate her, she couldn't have done a better job than Tibbie did.

Whenever anyone had an answer wrong, Tibbie's hand was in the air before the person even finished saying it. And her answer was always right too.

In science they talked about water birds.

They discussed the different kinds of birds that lived about the bay or migrated through or wintered there . . . ducks and coots and herons and egrets.

"We have two kinds of pelicans," Peter added. "White ones and the brown ones that dive from way up in the air to catch fish."

"The white ones have the biggest wings of any bird," Douglas said knowingly. "They're broader across than my Dad is tall even."

"But that's not the biggest," Tibbie said right out without holding up her hand.

"So who's got bigger wings than six and a half feet?" Douglas scoffed. "Miss Know-it-all!"

"The albatross," Tibbie said hotly. "The wandering albatross has wings almost twice that wide."

"Twelve feet! You've got to be kidding," he sneered.

Miss Barrow sighed and checked the bird book.

"The wandering albatross," she read after a minute. "Wing span the largest of any modern bird, up to eleven and a half feet." Then before anyone could speak, she became very stern. "There will be no more rudeness in these discussions. If you can't be polite, don't say anything."

Tibbie sat frowning darkly while they talked about grebes and shearwaters. Then Marianne mentioned petrels.

"It lays its eggs out on the Farallons," she said. "In little burrows."

"One egg," Tibbie corrected, quietly and sternly.

Miss Barrow sighed. "One egg to a bird," she said, glancing at the clock. "Tibbie, you must have a real bird expert in your family."

"I have a chart in my room," Tibbie said. "It has all the birds on it and all about them."

"In her room," Jeremy repeated aloud. "*Actually*, she lives in the museum."

"Her room *is* the museum," somebody added. Linda giggled and Tibbie flushed.

The rap of Miss Barrow's little tapper on the desk stopped the talk about birds.

"Remember this is Thursday," she said. "You might want to glance over your spelling words during the noon recess. Let's see if we can dislodge Linda from the throne." She smiled warmly at Linda as she said it, and Maggie knew that Linda was smiling back, looking smug and secure.

Because of what her brother Jason had said, Maggie went over specially to invite Tibbie for lunch.

"I have to eat somewhere," Tibbie said with a shrug.

"You don't have to eat with me," Maggie replied, feeling cross. "I just asked you."

"Of course I do," Tibbie said, looking at her squarely. "We're the only outsiders."

Maggie wanted to turn around and walk away right then but she couldn't do it, not with Tibbie staring at her like that.

"What if I asked you because I really wanted to?" Maggie said hotly.

"Okay," Tibbie said hesitantly. "Let's go."

"You sure do know a lot about birds," Maggie said after they set their lunches out. "Even if I had a whole room full of charts, I'm not sure I would remember those things."

"I mean to know everything someday," Tibbie said. "Someday."

"But it's not enough to be smart, you have to be wise too. That's what my brother Jason says."

Tibbie stared at Maggie, then laughed shortly. "So what does your brother know? If you are smart enough, you'll be wise all right."

"You're smart enough, but you're not wise enough to keep from making everybody mad at you about it," Maggie replied angrily.

"That's pretty rude," Tibbie said crossly.

"Look who's talking about rude!" Maggie said boldly. "If you were ever polite to me, I wouldn't be rude. I almost never am rude."

Tibbie stared at Maggie a minute and then held out her red apple. "Here," she said almost roughly.

Maggie grinned, glad that the tenseness of the moment was gone.

"I'm brave, too," she kidded. "I'll even take a red apple from a witch, but only if you'll share my cookies. Today they're chocolate chip."

"Two, if you insist," Tibbie said solemnly, picking them out. "Witches always take things in twos on Thursday."

Maggie looked to see if Tibbie were spoofing. But Tibbie's eyes stared dreamily off across the schoolyard to the mountain beyond for all the world as if she could see right through it to where petrels laid their eggs (one to a bird, of course) in the burrows on the Farallons.

# ❧ The Fall

When the bell rang, Maggie had forgotten even to take the spelling list out of her pocket. She tugged at it frantically as she and Tibbie raced for the door. Spelling contests made Maggie's stomach hurt and the letters always came out of her mouth in the wrong order, like kids getting out of line in a fire drill.

Maggie glanced only a moment at the corner of the blackboard where LINDA was written in gold-colored chalk. The name of the winner was always printed there until the next week. Linda's name had been in that box since the very beginning of the year. Until the day before, Maggie had been proud of it like Linda and the others, but now the letters of Linda's name seemed to tilt and sneer at her every time she looked at the board.

The patches of sunlight moved farther across the floor as the spellers went down.

All the words on their list were finally used up and Miss Barrow got out a list of new and harder words.

Maggie went down on "chocolate" by putting too many *a*'s in it.

Tibbie just kept on going.

Finally there was only one person left standing in each row and then there were only Tibbie and Linda at opposite ends of the room. They both spelled carefully, repeating the words and then spelling them out in syllables if they were long enough.

"The next word is eon," Miss Barrow said to Tibbie. "Eon . . . an indefinitely long period of time."

"A-E-O-N," Tibbie spelled carefully.

Miss Barrow glanced up and shook her head. Then she turned to Linda. "Eon, Linda, an indefinitely long period of time."

"E-O-N," Linda said in triumph, glancing toward Tibbie in a show-off way.

"That's not fair," Tibbie spoke up quickly. "Both spellings are right."

Miss Barrow frowned a moment, then said, "We'll see."

There was buzzing and some giggling as Miss Barrow opened the big dictionary to check. Linda smiled, her lips straightish and her head very high. Maggie wanted to slap her.

"E-O-N," Miss Barrow read aloud. "The other spelling is given but this one is first."

"But if you looked it up under the other spelling, that one would be listed second," Tibbie said. "So neither is wrong."

Miss Barrow glanced at Tibbie, checked the other spelling, and put the book away on its shelf. "Today we have *two* golden winners," she said, getting the eraser.

There was a great deal of buzzing and some very angry looks from Linda and the others as Linda's name was erased for the first time since the beginning of school. There really wasn't room in the space for two names so when Miss Barrow had finished, the names didn't look nearly so important, with the smaller letters cramped in there so tight.

Tibbie looked so forlorn in that last seat in the second row that Maggie turned around and winked at her, not caring who saw.

The recess bell sounded before Maggie could get turned back around, and the class rushed for the door.

"Good for you," Maggie said softly, catching up with Tibbie at the door. But Tibbie didn't smile. She let Maggie catch her hand and pull her along to the playground but she didn't look very happy.

"Maybe that was smarter than it was wise," she said glumly as Maggie tugged her along.

"Let's do the merry-go-round," Maggie said brightly. "We never have."

Tibbie wasn't exactly hanging back but she was thoughtful and funny. Timmy and Peter already had the merry-go-round spinning. Peter was running on the outside, pushing very hard to get it going fast. Maggie jumped on first and caught a support and called back to Tibbie.

"Run, Tibbie," she called. "Jump on."

Tibbie hesitated as the merry-go-round passed her one full turn. Then as Maggie watched, Tibbie crouched down a little to make a spring. As she squatted like that, the hem of her long dress lay on the cinders of the schoolyard. Maggie, watching, saw Linda put her foot out and pin down the hem of Tibbie's dress just as Tibbie started her jump.

"No, Linda, no," Maggie screamed. But it was too late.

All in one desperate moment Maggie saw Linda's triumphant smile; she saw Tibbie leap into the air and fall back heavily so that the spinning merry-go-round caught her sharply across the side of her head.

Suddenly the whole schoolyard was very still. Strangely, Maggie, unable to move, heard the wistful cry of a towhee from a nearby bush. Tibbie lay very still on the cinders with masses of dark hair all about her face and not moving at all.

Then everything began to happen. Maggie ran to Tibbie and she heard herself crying and shouting all at once. Linda was standing there looking very like a fish with her mouth open. Maggie shoved Linda so hard that she fell back against her friends. "You hurt her. You really hurt her bad, Linda," Maggie was shouting, not caring who heard, not caring what anyone thought.

As she leaned over Tibbie, Maggie heard people shouting for the teacher who was on yard duty and she felt the crowd drawing around them on running feet, but all that mattered was Tibbie.

Maggie gently pushed back Tibbie's dark shiny hair and saw the slow trickle of blood next to Tibbie's closed eyes.

Miss Barrow let Maggie tag along when they carried Tibbie into the nurse's office and laid her on the cot.

Even the grown-ups seemed awfully upset as they looked at Tibbie stretched out so tiny and so still on that bed.

"We must contact her parents right away," the nurse said, bathing the wound carefully with a sterile cloth.

"We have no home address yet," Miss Hopkins was telling the nurse unhappily. "Only a post office box."

"Telephone?" the nurse asked crisply. "Doctor's name?"

"She only came yesterday," Miss Hopkins explained unhappily.

"I know where she lives," Maggie said suddenly, in a funny scared voice. "I'll get somebody."

She turned and started out. Someone followed her. She thought it might be Miss Hopkins but she didn't turn around to see. Tibbie needed help, she needed a doctor and there was no other way.

She heard someone shout about taking her but it wasn't that far. Maggie cut across the corner of the schoolyard and started toward the mountain road.

She hadn't run more than a couple of blocks when she had to slow down and catch her breath. What would she say when she got there? She thought of how that little road looked from the car, so dark and scary, and she got a hard fearful place in her chest.

Then she began to run again so she couldn't think about it anymore.

# ❧ *The House Among the Trees*

Maggie knew the ocean road better than she knew any road in Marin County. Ever since she could remember, she had traveled over this road on the way to the beach with a huge basket of lunch and the sand castle toys and a frisbee to throw for Jefferson Dog.

After the road left the heart of Mill Valley, it wound over the folds of Mount Tamalpais and then snaked down the cliffs to the huge crescent of sand and stone that was Stinson Beach.

But Maggie had never walked the hill road. The giant eucalyptus trees towered above her, their trunks reddish where the bark had peeled away. The sun was high above her, and it seemed dark as Maggie, at a kind of half-trot, turned off the big road to go back among the trees.

This road was not smooth and firm like the big road. It was deeply dug with ruts and wound about lazily through huge masses of wild licorice. As Maggie brushed against their feathery strength, the air smelled like candy.

Then Maggie reached the final turn. The house rose before her like some great lumpy creature that had tumbled down for a nap, pulling its porches and chimneys in about it for warmth.

Around the corner of the house Maggie could see more buildings back among the trees, a separate garage and something that looked like a ramshackle stable, and then clear at the back, a great barn with a pointed top. It looked just like a storybook barn except that it wasn't red. Instead, it was the same streaked color that sea fog turns things after a while.

Maggie's footsteps rattled on the porch stairs and her heart sounded almost as loud. She was very frightened but she had to get help for Tibbie. From inside the house she could hear the faint whine of a small motor and then the soft humming of a tune she didn't recognize. From somewhere a woman's voice came softly in snatches as if she were thinking about something besides her song.

The instant that Maggie rapped at the door, a dog began to bark fiercely inside and a man called to silence it with a rough voice. After a minute the door opened and a man stared down at her.

He was ever so much taller than Jason, and he didn't smile at Maggie at all. He just waited. His long dark hair was caught back in a kind of pony tail. He had a short beard shaped like a box and was shirtless. Instead of a belt he wore a wide band of embroidery in all sorts of deep reds and purplish tones.

Maggie spoke as quickly as she could and was sorry that her voice sounded so scary and wavery.

"Virginia. I have to get Virginia," she blurted out.

The expression on the man's face changed strangely and he turned to the young woman who had come to stand behind him, watching Maggie.

She ran forward on quick bare feet and knelt in front of Maggie.

"What do you mean, child? Who are you? Why are you here?"

Maggie fought a sudden impulse to cry.

"Tibbie," Maggie said quickly. "Tibbie was hurt something awful at school and the nurse . . ."

The young woman seemed to stop listening and Maggie's words trailed off into the air.

"The car," she said to the man. "Quickly, Bill."

Within only minutes the three of them were in a square bus hurtling along the rutted stretch of road. The girl, whose name Maggie still didn't know, put a hand on Maggie's knee to brace her as Bill fought the wheel along the rough track.

"You'll have to direct him," the young woman said, as Bill charged the bus onto the main road.

"And a doctor," Bill finally spoke. "What if she needs a doctor?"

"My doctor is a really nice man," Maggie said shyly. "And he likes kids like us, too."

The girl patted Maggie's knee again without looking down at her. "That's good, child," she said gently. "We'll see."

A straggle of kindergartners were leaving the school grounds as the bus stopped in the drive. Other than that, everyone was in class for the last short session before dismissal.

From the outer office, Maggie could see that both the principal and the assistant principal were crowded into the room with the nurse and Tibbie.

"Do you mind waiting?" the young woman asked Maggie. "About the doctor?"

Maggie shook her head. She didn't mind, but she did feel strange being there in the office when everyone else was in class.

Maggie followed as Bill carried Tibbie out like a small precious doll and laid her in the young woman's lap. Maggie climbed into the back seat of the bus with Miss Hopkins still watching them from the door.

Tibbie looked dazed and dreamy. Her hair was pasted down where the nurse had washed it clean and set a temporary bandage over the wound.

"You're missing class," Tibbie said dreamily to Maggie.

"I know," Maggie replied, smiling at her.

Tibbie's lashes dropped again and a small pucker of hurt showed around her mouth. There was silence in the bus except for Maggie's driving directions.

A mother in a pink pantsuit holding a little girl by the hand was just leaving Dr. Hamilton's office. Maggie went right up to the nurse and told her about Tibbie's accident. Dr. Hamilton let the young woman take Tibbie right on in even though there were people waiting in the outside room.

Bill and Maggie waited silently among the magazines and the playthings along with the other people.

Maggie thought Dr. Hamilton was keeping Tibbie in there an awfully long time. Other patients came and looked at their watches and then sighed and waited. It must have seemed like a long time to Bill, because he stirred restlessly in the chair that wasn't nearly big enough for him. Finally he turned to Maggie.

"Maybe I should have taken you back to school."

"I want to see how Tibbie is," she told him.

He stared at her and then frowned a little. "You're a cool one," he said as if he thought that was a good thing to be.

Maggie grinned just a little. "Not really," she admitted. "I was scared."

"For Tibbie?" he asked.

She nodded.

"What happened?" he asked.

"She hit her head on the merry-go-round," Maggie explained.

He shook his head. "That's pretty strange. She's a goat—never falls."

"A girl made her fall," Maggie explained. "By standing on her dress when she jumped."

"On purpose?" he asked.

Maggie nodded. "She was jealous."

"Poor Tibbie," he said slowly, staring down at his great broad hands. "She learns slow."

"She's awful smart," Maggie defended quickly.

He looked at her and smiled a twitch. "In studies maybe," he agreed slowly.

"Is that girl with her Virginia?" Maggie asked.

"No," he said shortly. There was something in his face that kept Maggie from talking to him anymore and they waited together in silence.

Dr. Hamilton came clear out into the waiting room with Tibbie when he was through examining her. He smiled when he saw Maggie and reached over and gave her a small hug, leaving his arm lightly on her shoulder.

"A slight concussion, no fracture," he announced, speaking to Bill, who had risen and seemed to fill the air of the room with his immense size. "That means her head is cracked but not broken, Magpie!" he added to Maggie, smiling reassuringly. Then he spoke to Bill again.

"She ought to be well enough to go back to school by Monday, barring complications. She's going to have a whale of a headache and at least one black eye, but she'll be a good sport about it, won't you?"

Tibbie smiled weakly back at him and they started to leave.

"Tell your folks 'Hi' for me, Magpie," Dr. Hamilton added to Maggie with a wink as he started back down the hall.

Maggie shook her head when Bill offered her a ride home.

"Thanks, Maggie," Tibbie said in a funny weak voice as the bus pulled away.

"See you tomorrow maybe," Maggie said, feeling not at all sure.·

Maggie cut through the schoolyard on the way home. A bunch of boys were playing baseball on the diamond at the end of the play yard and an older man was hitting a small ball against the side of the building with a slow steady rhythm.

Then she passed the merry-go-round. She didn't want to look at it for fear it would still have Tibbie's blood on it. Instead she looked at the cinders underneath as she walked by.

That was when she saw it. In among the reddish cinders of the schoolyard surface was a round stone. It was grayish and kind of blue.

She leaned over and picked it up. The funniest little feeling went all over her when she saw the strange symbol gleaming from her palm. It was Tibbie's seven stone that was supposed to protect her from things and that she wouldn't part with for anything in the whole wide world. But Tibbie had lost it and now she would be scared and unhappy without it.

Almost afraid of the stone, Maggie slipped it into her pocket and ran all the rest of the way home.

# ❧ *Virginia*

Maggie could hardly wait to get there to talk to Jason. But when she got home, DeeDee Barkley from down the street was waiting instead. DeeDee was her baby sitter. She was just Jason's age and very pretty. She was arranging cookies on a tray when Maggie ran in.

"Intramural basketball," DeeDee explained. "And you better cross your fingers that the sophomores win too!"

Maggie nodded and went to her room. She put the seven stone in the bottom drawer of the little cardboard chest that Jason had brought her from Chinatown. She put the stone in upside down so the sign wouldn't show.

She took the cookies out in the yard to eat them with Jefferson Dog, who sat and wagged for bites until the last crumb was gone. Then Maggie threw a stick for him until he got tired and sat by her to think too.

When Maggie thought it might be five o'clock she went inside. DeeDee was watching television.

"It's after five," DeeDee explained. "Your mother called and said she would be late and your daddy would pick her up. She also said I should fix you early dinner if you wanted it."

"I'm not hungry," Maggie told her. "I'll wait."

When she went back outside, Jefferson Dog brought her the stick to show her that he was rested but she only threw it once.

Tibbie would feel awful when she realized that she had lost her seven stone. She might not even be able to get well without it. If Tibbie really believed that the stone protected her, she could be crying for it right now, this very minute, up there in the house among the trees.

The sun was all the way gone and the street lights were starting to come on when Maggie decided.

She knew she was right to take the stone to Tibbie but she was also pretty sure that DeeDee wouldn't let her go if she knew the truth.

She planned what to say exactly before she went back into the house.

"DeeDee," she said very casually, standing where DeeDee couldn't see her face without really twisting around in her chair.

"Changed your mind about dinner?" DeeDee asked easily, her knitting needles clicking a little behind her words.

"No, I just remembered that I have something of my friend's that she might need."

"Does she live close?"

"Pretty close," Maggie said, carefully.

"You wouldn't be gone very long?" DeeDee asked.

"I would run right there and run back," Maggie said.

"It's okay, I guess," DeeDee decided. "But be careful."

With the seven stone in her pocket, Maggie ran all the way to school and past and then on up the hill. The traffic was very heavy. All the people who lived on the hill were winding up toward their homes and dinner. She wasn't scared nearly as bad as she thought she would be.

Once a dog behind a fence barked suddenly as she passed and sometimes a car would slow down but those were the only scary things.

Then she turned off on the rutted road and saw dim lights shining from here and there among the trees.

For the first time Maggie really wondered if she had done the right thing. Her steps slowed as she approached the porch and she hoped very hard that nobody strange would open the door, that it would be the young woman or Bill or even Tibbie who answered her knock.

It was Bill who answered the door.

He peered out at her in the darkness and said, "What do you know . . . the Magpie."

Maggie flushed. Only people who had known her all her life, like her parents and Jason and Dr. Hamilton, ever called her that.

"Tibbie lost something," she said. "I brought it to her."

"She's back in her room," he said. Then, strangely, instead of inviting her in, he came out on the porch beside her and pulled the door shut behind him.

Maggie, very puzzled, followed his light steps around the house.

They passed the saggy garage and the stables that were dank-smelling from old hay and then Bill rapped loudly on a small door in the side of the barn.

The door was opened by the young woman that Maggie had seen earlier.

"Well, look here!" she cried. "You have company, Tibbie."

Maggie stared into the great open room of the barn. For that first moment she thought it was the most beautiful place she had ever seen in her whole life. There wasn't much furniture to speak of but it would have taken a whole carload of furniture to fill it anyway. The cement floor was swept clean. Over in the corner a giant lamp had been made from a huge milk can. By the lamp were some chairs and a bed where Tibbie was sitting up, books all around her and a huge stuffed bear staring one-eyed at her from the foot.

But it was the room itself that was fantastic. There were bright full-color maps nailed along the walls between the bookcases. And hundreds of books! Hundreds of books, Maggie realized, her eyes wide with wonder. Puppets hung smiling and scowling from nails along the wall and a great doll house of heavy cardboard stood beneath them.

There were circus posters, and a chart of all the dogs in the world and where they came from. There was the map of weather that Tibbie had mentioned, and a huge chart of shells, and another one of sailing boats. There was every kind of map that Maggie could imagine and then some more.

From the top of a great wine barrel, dolls seemed to be pushing up to see what was going on. Maggie thought that she could have played in that room for a whole year and never run out of things to look at or do.

Then she looked up. The trap door in the ceiling was tied open and against the deep blue sky a single first star shone into Tibbie's room.

When Maggie looked down again, her eyes met Tibbie's. Maggie gasped. Her lovely small face was swollen on the side where she had been hit and looked reddened and sore. But Tibbie didn't seem to realize or care how she looked.

"I'm so glad you came," Tibbie said, pushing the knitted blanket off her knees. "I feel so great now that I could play."

"No sir!" the young woman said firmly. "Not tonight."

"I can't stay anyway," Maggie said, fishing in her pocket. "I just thought I would bring you this."

She handed the seven stone to Tibbie. "I found it on the playground," she explained quietly.

Tibbie seized the stone and held it tightly in both her hands. "Oh," she cried. "Oh. Oh."

The young woman chuckled softly. She reached out and touched Maggie softly on the shoulder. "I think she means 'Thanks!' "

But Tibbie's eyes were very bright as if she were going to cry. She just held the stone in her hands and said nothing.

"Now I have to go," Maggie said, after a moment.

"Not right away," the girl said, surprised.

Maggie nodded. "I really kind of sneaked off," she admitted.

The young woman glanced up at the dark sky which had somehow gotten three more stars since Maggie looked before. "I bet you did. It's really dark for you to be away from home. You can stay with Tibbie a minute and then Bill will drive you home. It will come out to the same amount of time."

"I really shouldn't," Maggie hesitated.

"But Tibbie has something for you," the girl said, looking over at Tibbie who still stood with the stone tight in her hands. "Haven't you, Tibbie?"

"Can I get it?" Tibbie asked. "Do you think it is ready?"

The girl frowned. "You shouldn't really be hopping about. Doesn't that make your headache worse?"

Tibbie shook her head carefully. "It's ever so much better now."

The girl studied Tibbie's face a minute and then smiled gently. "Okay. But take it easy. We'll wait here. There's no rush."

The minute Tibbie walked through the big barn door and closed it behind her, the girl turned to Maggie. She took both Maggie's hands loosely and looked at Maggie right in the eyes.

"Listen, Maggie," she said softly. "I have something I must tell you because you are Tibbie's friend."

Maggie, her heart thumping for no reason at all, looked into the girl's face and waited.

"Bill said that you asked him about Virginia."

Maggie nodded. "Tibbie talks about Virginia a lot. I thought that might be you."

The girl shook her head slowly. "I'm Carole." Then she added slowly, "There is no Virginia here."

"But I don't understand," Maggie said.

"Virginia is Tibbie's mother, but she is gone."

"Dead?" Maggie asked numbly.

Carole shook her head slowly. "Not dead, Maggie, just gone. Virginia is—well, she's different, and wonderful, and very restless.

She went away one time and didn't come back." Carole paused to let Maggie understand. But Maggie didn't understand.

"But how could a mother just go away from a little girl?" she asked slowly, feeling a hollow place of fear deep inside.

"That's what Tibbie asks herself all the time, Maggie," Carole said gently. "And she can't accept that Virginia would leave her like that. That's why she studies more than she should, and wants to know more than anyone else even if it makes her lonely and disliked. She wants to be so *good* and so *wonderful* that Virginia will want her and come back."

"And you just take care of her?" Maggie asked, looking about at that marvelous room. "And love her like she was yours?"

"She is ours and we are hers," Carole said gently, "because we love her. Even as you are her friend and she is yours because you like each other."

Maggie stared at Carole. It seemed to her that she had never seen any face as beautiful as Carole's, there in that almost dark room.

"I wanted you to understand about Tibbie so you would know how important it was for her to have her seven stone back. Not because the stone is valuable, Maggie, but because you valued Tibbie enough to bring it to her."

Maggie turned as she heard the door open behind her.

"The paint is dry," Tibbie called to Carole with delight. Then she held her hand out to Maggie. "Look what I have for you."

Maggie took the small round stone and held it in her hand. It was just like Tibbie's seven stone except that the symbol on it was different. She stared at it, not knowing what to say.

"It will bring you all kinds of strength," Tibbie said eagerly. "Just like mine does."

Maggie raised her eyes to Tibbie and then looked past her to where Carole watched, her eyes warm and sad and pained all at once.

With the stone tight in her palm, Maggie threw her arms about Tibbie. She hugged her as close as she dared with that bandage and all. Tibbie smelled nice and clean with antiseptic, like Dr. Hamilton usually did. Her hair felt silky and Maggie heard her short, unbelieving intake of breath.

"Thank you, Tibbie," Maggie said breathlessly. "Thank you ever, ever, ever, so much."

Tibbie still looked dazed and funny as Maggie left with Bill for the rough ride back to her own house.

The porch light was on and DeeDee was cross with relief when Maggie opened the door.

Her mother and father and Jason all got there within minutes. Jason was excited because they had won the game and her mother was racing about to get dinner on. DeeDee didn't even stay long enough to tell on Maggie for being away so long.

"It's working," Maggie told herself. "My stone is already working because I didn't even get in Dutch."

She sat in the corner of the kitchen with one arm around Jefferson Dog and watched her mother go back and forth, first with salad greens and then with milk for the gravy. She thought about Tibbie and Virginia.

Maggie went to sleep that night with the stone under her pillow and something heavy and painful inside her chest.

# ❧ *The Long Weekend*

That next morning Maggie woke up with a scratchy throat and her nose was so snuffly that her voice came out funny.

She dressed very quickly for school, hoping that her mother wouldn't notice anything different. But when her mother set her plate in front of her she frowned slightly at Maggie.

"What's the matter with our Magpie?" her father asked, lowering his paper to peer at her. "She looks a little peaky to me."

"I'm fine," Maggie tried to say but it came out sounding more like "I'be fide."

Her mother laughed and laid a soft hand in the hollow of Maggie's neck under her ear like she always did to test for fever.

"That is a little hot box!" Maggie's mother said with surprise, pulling her hand away as if she were startled.

Her father rose and came around and felt her neck too and shook his head. "It's back into the pj's for you, Miss," he said gently. "You can't go outside like that."

Tears welled in Maggie's eyes. What if Tibbie came to school and there was nobody to be friends with her?

"No tears, honey," her mother said gently. "Mrs. Wells will come over and sit with you until Jason comes. I'll call Dr. Hamilton and he'll send out some medicine and by Monday . . ."

"Monday," Maggie wailed.

"Monday," her mother repeated firmly.

Mrs. Wells was old and round and smiling. She talked to herself when she didn't realize anyone was around. But mostly she sat and rocked back and forth and pulled a bone crochet hook through an endless string of thread, changing colors and working swiftly so that huge piles of small squares overflowed the basket she always carried with her.

Jason carried the TV into Maggie's room and she watched it for a while. But the medicine that Dr. Hamilton sent made her sleepy so that she mostly dozed and dressed and undressed her dolls and then dozed again.

Saturday morning her neck still felt hot so she stayed in bed and watched the cartoons. Jason brought his breakfast in to eat with her and they watched together.

Finally, during a commercial, Maggie got up courage enough to tell Jason about Tibbie.

He whistled softly when she was through telling him about the accident. "That's one ugly way for a little kid to treat another one."

Maggie nodded. The cartoon had started again but neither of them paid any attention to it.

Maggie told him about Dr. Hamilton and how nice he had been to Tibbie. "He'll make her well, I know he will."

Jason nodded. "You remember last year when Steve Cole got a concussion in football?"

Maggie nodded. "He got along fine," Jason assured her. "He had a whale of a headache for a long time but by the end of the season he was out there bashing himself around again."

"I was going over to see her," Maggie said unhappily. "I thought I'd take her a little present maybe, or at least a card."

Jason shook his head. "Not a chance with that cold of yours. And even if you had a card to send it wouldn't get there until Monday and you'll see her yourself by then."

Maggie sighed unhappily and stared at the TV without really seeing it.

Jason was quiet for a minute or two also; then he spoke suddenly in a kind of excited way. "Hey Magpie," he said happily. "I just had this real brainstorm. I could bring you paper and you could borrow my marking pencils and make her a card yourself. When you had it all done, I'd jog up there and take it to her. Then she'd KNOW you were thinking about her."

"You'd do that?" Maggie stared at him wide-eyed. "You really would? And you think I could make a card good enough?"

He didn't answer, he only grinned and punched her shoulder as he got up and went off for the drawing things.

Maggie drew a lot of pictures but none of them looked good enough or just right for Tibbie. She tried to write a poem about getting well but there were always too many words in the third line so that it lopped over and spoiled the look of the page.

Finally she took a nice clean new sheet of paper. She drew a square in the middle that was shaped like the window she remembered in the roof of Tibbie's room. She colored the whole square blue except for one single star that she left white, being very careful to keep its edges sharp and gleaming. Then she wrote across the top: "A WISH FOR MY FRIEND." At the bottom she wrote "GET WELL" in very big blue letters and signed it "Maggie."

Jason was brushing Jefferson Dog out on the back steps when Maggie finished the card. She put on her house slippers and her quilted robe and went out to show it to him.

He looked at it frowning and pulling his mouth down funny, as if he were a critic or something. Then he nodded and smiled at her in that kind of special way.

"That is a lucky little friend you have there," he said solemnly. "To get a handmade card like that and so pretty too."

Maggie looked at him carefully to see if he was making fun of her but from the way he ruffled her hair, she knew he wasn't and she hugged his words down inside herself.

"You know where she lives?" she asked, a little worried.

He nodded, rising and holding the card carefully. "I even have a mailing envelope to carry it in so it won't get all bent up."

It seemed to Maggie that Jason was gone an awfully long time. The cough syrup that Dr. Hamilton had sent tasted like cherries and made her so sleepy that she finally took a nap even though she meant to wait every minute until Jason got back.

She wakened to hear his voice in the living room. He was talking to her mother and his voice rose and fell with real excitement. Maggie leaped out of bed to join them.

"You can't believe the work that girl does, Mom," Jason was saying. "Not only is it as good as anything you ever see in a gift shop but she's original . . . really clever."

"Does she work with glazes only or with designs too?" Maggie's mother asked.

"Both," he said. Then he saw Maggie in the doorway and she went over and sat on the arm of his chair. "I was just telling Mom about the pottery that Trish does. It's really something else! Did you get to see any of it while you were there?"

Maggie shook her head. "I only went to Tibbie's room," she explained. She waited a minute but she couldn't stand it. "Did she like the card?"

"Did she ever!" Jason said. "She was so excited and surprised that I honestly thought she was going to bawl. She hugged it real tight and looked so funny that Carole—you know her I guess—suggested I might like to go look at the pottery. I think she did it so that Tibbie wouldn't be embarrassed by busting into tears in front of me."

"And is she all right?" Maggie asked.

Jason shook his head. "I think she's got a headache out of this world and she's got a shiner you wouldn't believe."

"Shiner?" Maggie asked in confusion.

"Black eye," Jason explained. "It's not only black though, it's also blue and yellow . . . a real colorful scene."

Maggie stared at him and her mother broke in quickly. "It will go away in no time, Maggie. It is perfectly natural for her eye to do that after a hard blow near it. But she'll be fine. Jason assured me of that."

"But I've never had a friend with a black eye before," Maggie said thoughtfully.

"You've never had a friend like Tibbie before," Jason reminded her. "That is one special little girl and you sure made her happy with that card of yours today."

Maggie only half listened as Jason told his mother about the designs of Trish's pottery, how she had somehow captured the feel of desert Indian work in forms that were just individual enough to add a whole new dimension to the art.

"Those things just glow with the sense of sun and sand and stones," he went on. "I asked Trish if she would mind coming down to school with a bunch of them. I know Mr. Prather would really like his pottery classes to see work of that quality with so much originality of design. She was shy about it but she did promise to come if he wanted her to. I'm going to talk to him about it first thing Monday."

"If somebody else is going to go back to school Monday she had better high-tail her little pajamas back into that bed," Maggie's mother cautioned with a grin.

Maggie crawled back into her bed feeling all warm and cozy inside. Jefferson Dog tagged after her and, after turning around a few times, settled down for a nap on her little rug.

Maggie didn't even turn the TV set on again. She just lay and thought about Tibbie and how she had almost cried with happiness when she got the card. And she thought about Jason too, proudly somehow, as if his excitement about Tibbie and the pottery was something nice and reassuring between herself and Tibbie. She liked it when Jason liked her friends. She liked thinking about Tibbie's friend Trish going down to Jason's big high school and showing them something new and wonderful about pottery.

And she liked herself a little bit more too, runny nose and all.

Then finally it was Sunday and her temperature was normal and she didn't have to have a tissue in her hand every minute and she knew for sure that she would get to go back to school on Monday.

# ৪৫ *The Seven Stone*

Maggie left the stone that Tibbie had given her under her pillow until she was all ready for school Monday morning. But when her milk money was in her sack and her card inside her library book, she went back and got the stone.

She stared at its perfect roundness in her hand. The mysterious sign glowed from the stone's face. When she turned the stone over, she could feel it losing its coldness in the secretness of her fist. Slipping it into her jumper pocket, she left for school in a hurry before she could change her mind about taking it with her.

But she thought about the stone all the way to school. If you weren't a witch and never wanted to be a witch (in fact really wanted to be an airline stewardess when you grew up), would a seven stone make any difference to you? She wished she had had the courage to show the stone to Jason when she was telling him about Tibbie's accident. But since she was afraid to tell him about her trip to the house in the woods, she hadn't mentioned it to him.

She imagined she could feel the stone's weight in her pocket and hear Tibbie's voice, low and persuasive.

The playground was loud with shouting boys. Whirls of color glinted from the spinning merry-go-round. Surely Tibbie would be back to school today, Maggie thought, looking around the playground for her eagerly. At first she didn't even notice Linda and the others, all clustered together in a bright little group by the door.

But Linda called out to her.

"Hi, Maggie," she said warmly. "We're over here."

They were all looking at her and smiling, waiting for her to come and join them. She stumbled a little, her feet dragging in spite of herself and that funny knot of hurt starting inside her chest.

How could anybody hate you on Thursday and then say "Hi, Maggie, we're over here," on the very next Monday?

But they were all waiting and there was nothing to do but walk slowly toward them, all by herself.

"We just haven't been able to wait," Linda said in that kind of voice that shares a secret. "Tell us where you went . . . to that new girl's place. What was it like?"

Maggie stood silent a minute. She was there, inside that circle with Linda and the others, where she wanted to be so much. But somehow being there wasn't nice at all. She felt like a big frosty bun being passed about among them on a plate. She slid her hand inside her pocket and felt the cool perfection of the stone slide inside her fist.

The coolness of the stone seemed to move all through her. She felt taller and straighter than she could ever remember.

"Tibbie's house?" she said quietly. "It was just great . . . that's all."

"What kind of a place is it?" Linda asked impatiently. "Like our houses or is it all hippie with signs and the old trucks and things?"

Maggie could feel every bit of that stone inside her hand.

"It's a lot bigger than my own house," she said right out. "And set way back in the trees. With hundreds of books in her room and maps and charts and everything she said . . . and puppets too."

They were glancing at each other, Linda and the others, in a helpless, annoyed way.

"Oh, come on, Maggie," Linda said with irritation. "You don't have to defend that girl."

"Somebody better defend her," Maggie said hotly. "If you're going to go around half-killing anyone that's smarter than you. And if you need ugly things to say about Tibbie, you don't have to get them from me. You can just make them up out of your own head like you do about other people. Like Betty Ann, and me." Suddenly Maggie choked on her own words. She was shouting and other people were looking, but she couldn't help it, she had to say the rest.

"She's got the greatest room in the whole world, that's all. In the greatest house with the greatest people and besides that, she's my friend."

"Well," Linda said, pulling back with a funny scared little look. "How do you like that?" she asked her friends.

"I like it fine," the low voice came behind Maggie. Maggie turned to stare at Tibbie, who was looking at Linda very cool and straight in spite of her huge black eye (that had begun to turn yellow around the edges) and the white bandage on her head.

Linda looked away. She couldn't meet Tibbie's glance. In fact, she turned clear around, her blonde hair swaying. She tugged at Shelley's arm. She was almost running.

But Shelley shook her arm free. The others stayed too, looking awkward and embarrassed.

"I'm sorry about what happened," Shelley said softly. "We talked about it, and we really are."

Tibbie studied Shelley and the others a minute with her hard dark eyes and then she put a hand on Shelley's arm.

"I'm sorry I was so show-offy. I guess I asked for it—kind of."

Then there were just the two of them, Maggie and Tibbie, all alone. Tibbie smiled. Maggie had never seen Tibbie really smile before and suddenly she was beautiful, all warmth and bubbly with a funny little dimple that came quick and stayed in her left cheek below where the bruise stopped.

Then Tibbie laughed. It was a hearty laugh that showed all her white teeth. She seized Maggie's hands and began to jump up and down in her awkward little boots. Maggie's lunch and her books fell to the ground but Tibbie didn't even look down.

"It worked, Maggie," she squealed. "Your stone worked just like mine. Carole was right. Carole was really right. You do have your stone, don't you?"

Maggie nodded, feeling the weight of the stone in her pocket.

The ring of the bell came loudly in Maggie's ears and she started to pick up her things. Children streamed by them toward the building but Tibbie held Maggie tight, her dark eyes dancing.

"I wasn't sure. I thought Virginia had to make it, or at least it had to have your birth sign. But Carole said I was wrong. She said it wasn't the stone that did the magic, it was the believing."

"But I don't understand."

"Get it out," Tibbie danced. "Let me show you. A real seven stone is a witch's thing. Carole said you weren't a witch any more than I am. She said you were just a sweet small person who didn't know how great you were just being yourself."

"But the sign?" Maggie asked, staring at it.

"It's your own sign all right," Tibbie giggled. "Look at it. It is really an M for Maggie put on top of a U for Underwood. That's all you needed, Carole said, just to hang on tight to being Maggie Underwood. And it worked."

The teacher welcomed Tibbie back so cordially that it seemed to make all the other kids in the class act friendlier too.

"Are you all right now?" Miss Barrow asked gently.

"Everything is perfect," Tibbie said in a gentle voice that even Maggie hadn't heard Tibbie use before. Then she added, "Thank you very much."

Her bright eyes strayed to Maggie and they both grinned. Maggie's hand closed over her stone. "My own strength," she thought proudly. "My very own."

Maybe Jason would let her borrow his magic markers again and make a beautiful sign like that on the front of her book bag, for everyone to see but nobody to understand.

But even if he didn't, she would have that stone of her ownness warm from Carole's belief. Round and warm and perfect.

And a best friend named Tibbie.